Travel to Maurice's World!

Maurice's World is your passport to adventure—online. Explore other books in the *Maurice's Valises* series. Make friends from all over the world. Earn moral badges and collect treasures from Maurice's travels. Create your own Moral Scrolls and play fun games. Plus, stamp your virtual passport using the special code below. And there's more to come soon, including a valise hunt!

Visit mauricesvalises.com

YOUR SPECIAL CODE IS **TRUTH**

ISBN: 9789491613036-51695

MOUSE PRINTS PRESS
Prinsengracht 1053-S Boot
1017 JE Amsterdam Netherlands

"Call me Maurice," said Grandpa Maurice, adjusting his woolly muffler. Then he sat himself down in his storytelling chair—his favorite because it was lumpy, and the lumps were all in the right places.

He sat by the hearth surrounded by his ninety-eight grandmice and some of their forest friends.

And they all sat in Maurice's living room, warm and cozy, deep in the woods, in the base of an old sycamore tree.

Book I:

...in the base of an old sycamore tree.

Maurice's Valises

Moral Tails in an Immoral World

Book I:
In The Beginning

By J.S. Friedman

Illustrations by Chris Beatrice

They had gathered to hear Maurice retell one of his famous traveling tales.

A fire crackled in the fireplace.

A winter wind howled outside.

And snow danced and swept the ground clean and white.

"Grandpa Maurice," came a voice from somewhere in back, "tell us how it all began."

"Ahhh, that one." Maurice sighed, sorting through the stacks and stacks of stories in his head. "But first tell me, which one are you?"

"Oh, Grandpa, it's me—Leopold! Your eldest grandmouse."

Maurice winked knowingly. Then he turned to the stack of worn valises behind him. The topmost almost touched the ceiling.

Each had a label and was covered with stickers from the place where Maurice had traveled with it.

Each was packed with memories and special things Maurice wanted to keep.

PAW NOTE

A valise is an old-fashioned piece of luggage used for traveling.

And to Maurice, each was like an old friend.

Maurice got up and poked around until he found the right valise.

He jiggled it a little this way; he jiggled it a little that way until he finally pulled it out from the pile.

But when he tried to open it, it wouldn't open.

So he tugged on the latch until it popped.

Out fell a piece of coconut shell, an old curl of wool from the coat of a sheep and, of course, a scroll. But not just any scroll—a Moral Scroll.

With these in hand, Maurice settled back into his comfy chair and began his tale.

PAW NOTE

A Moral Scroll is a paper with a wise saying written on it.
The saying is the lesson learned from a particular traveling tale.

"Let's see now…It all started with my first memory…
I distinctly remember a female's soft voice in the air:
'Maurice? Maurice? Can you hear me, Maurice?
Maurice is your name little one.'

I looked right.

I looked left.

I sniffed the air.

But saw no one—all there was, was me. A newborn mouse
riding in a coconut shell, rocked by ocean waves."

"Then I heard the voice again. 'Maurice…I am the Muse of Mice, the voice of the Then, the Now, and the Later…

You will always be able to hear me. I'll always watch over you. You are a special mouse.'

You know," said Maurice, "even though these were the first words I ever heard, I understood them.

Even though I was tiny.

Even though I was new.

Even though no one else was there."

"I continued riding and rocking in my coconut shell, but then—Slosh! Bump! Kaplop!

My coconut shell bumped against the shore. And the next thing I knew, I was dumped on the sand!

'Maurice…Maurice, get up,' cried the voice of the Muse.

I stumbled up on my shaky legs.

I stepped on my ears.

Then I fell into a hole, or what I thought was a hole.

But it was no hole.

It was a giant mouse paw print in the sand!"

"'Maurice,' said the Muse, 'you have been allowed to fall into the sacred mouse paw print. You are destined to become the new moral compass for all mice.

That means you will grow up and travel to many distant lands,' said the voice. 'And as you travel and see what you will see, you must pass your learning down to other mice.'"

"'It will be your duty to save all the travel tales and wise lessons. You will write these lessons on Moral Scrolls for others to learn from. And each tale and its Moral Scroll must be kept in its own valise. Just as other special mice have done before you.

You will become Maurice of the Valise...'"

"Then the voice was gone. Only the whisper of the ocean remained.

The first wise lesson I was to pass on came from my first adventure, which began only minutes after my step into and out of the sacred mouse paw print.

There I was, just sniffing the air, when I sniffed something wonderful. Cheese. Glorious cheese!

I followed my nose up a nearby hill."

"The climb was hard. I hadn't yet grown into my ears or my tail and had to drag them along the ground.

When I reached the top, I found a shepherd boy. (I later learned his name was Samuel.) He was sitting on the grass eating bread and cheese. Sheep were grazing all around him. And I could see a small village below."

"I was about to check if any of the shepherd boy's cheese had fallen on the ground when, suddenly, I heard a piercing voice shout, 'Skunk, Skunk!'

I ran behind a rock.

The sheep ran down to the village.

And Samuel the shepherd boy ran after them.

But we had all been tricked.

When I peered around the rock, I saw a mountain rat nibbling a piece of the fallen bread as he watched the sheep scatter. (I later learned his name was Ratty.) The mountain rat fell on the ground and rolled with laughter.

Still hungry, I decided to take advantage of the commotion, so I ran to get some crumbs myself."

"'Scram, baby mouse! Get your own food,' yelled the mountain rat. Quickly, he gathered all the bread and cheese he could carry and scurried up the hill, snickering as he went.

The sheep returned with Samuel the shepherd boy. There had been no skunk. The sheep, shaking their heads in disgust, grumbled that they had been tricked.

The villagers didn't know the mountain rat made the sheep scatter. They shook their heads in disgust too and grumbled that the boy was not a good shepherd.

Even the shepherd boy shook his head in disgust. He grumbled that the mountain rat was making trouble for him."

"A few minutes later, as I was looking in the grass for any bread or cheese crumbs, a big stone rolled by and almost hit me.

Startled, I ran and hid behind a sleeping sheep. I peeked from around its wooly curls and—guess what?

Atop the hill stood Ratty. He was laughing because he had pushed the stone that made me jump.

The sheep bleated a warning:

'Baaaah, the mountain rat is bored.'

'Baaaah, he's a nasty nasty.'

'Baaaah, baa careful.'"

"As the afternoon wore on, I decided to take a short mouse-nap in the grass alongside the sheep.

Suddenly, I woke to hear, 'Fire! Fire! The hay is burning!'

Behind a haystack, smoke curled into the air. The sheep scattered and ran down the hill. And the shepherd boy ran to put out the fire.

When Samuel reached the haystack, he found the mountain rat cooking some cheese."

"Ratty looked up, laughed, and scampered off to see if the shepherd boy had left any more food behind.

He had fooled the shepherd boy again.

He had fooled the sheep again.

And he had fooled the villagers into thinking that Samuel the shepherd boy could not take care of the sheep, again."

"This time, when Samuel got home, the villagers told him, 'We will not allow you to be shepherd boy if you can't take care of the sheep.'

Samuel and his sheep trudged back up the hill, determined not to be fooled again.

That night, as the moon came shining up, the sheep huddled together on the side of the hill, gossiping."

"Once again, I was snuggled into the curly wool of one sheep, listening contentedly as sheep gossip slowly turned into sheep snores.

Even Ratty the mountain rat was rolled up in his blanket under the moon, ready to sleep."

"But, all of a sudden, the sheep became alert!

There were frantic sheep whispers.

They sensed something.

Smelled something.

Heard something.

They began to 'baaaah!'

A hungry skunk had hunted down the cheese Ratty was hoarding."

"When Ratty saw the danger, he cried, 'Skunk! Skunk! Help, there is a hungry skunk!'

The sheep heard his cry. But this time they did not run.

Again Ratty yelled, 'Help! Help! There really is a skunk! He's after my food!'

But the sheep still didn't move. The sheep didn't believe him.

Samuel opened his eyes, but he didn't move. Samuel didn't believe him.

Even I didn't move. I didn't believe him.

So the skunk ran after Ratty and his cheese.

That was it."

"Except that Ratty the mountain rat, who wouldn't let go of his food, ran as fast as he could over the hill, being chased by the skunk.

Neither was ever seen again.

All of us went back to bed.

I lay back down.

The shepherd boy lay back down.

And the sheep lay back down.

And, of course, they began to snore."

The End

When Maurice finished the story of "The Rat Who Cried Skunk," there was a long silence in the room.

Then Leopold spoke up.

"Grandpa Maurice, what is the lesson? What does the Moral Scroll say?"

Maurice slowly unrolled the scroll that had come from his valise. It was old, full of holes, and looked like a slice of Swiss cheese.

Maurice turned it around for all to see as he read it out loud:

There is no believing a liar,
even when he speaks
the truth

Everyone was quiet as each chewed over this thought. You could have heard a mouse whisper.

Maurice looked at his grandmice and their friends.

All the grandmice and their friends looked at each other.

But before anyone could ask another question, Maurice's eyes began to close.

And just that fast, he began to snore. And believe it or not, it sounded just like sheep snores.

The end, again.
(*But more to come…*)

map of
Maurice's
Travels

North America

South America

Europe

Asia

Africa

Australia

"A liar will not be believed, even when he speaks the truth."

–*Aesop*

History repeats itself and so do its stories. Aesop (620-560 BC) was a slave in ancient Greece who is known for his collection of fables, known as *Aesop's Fables*.

One of his most famous fables is *The Boy Who Cried Wolf*, a tale about a shepherd boy who repeatedly tricks villagers into thinking a wolf is attacking his flock. When a wolf actually does appear, the villagers do not believe him, and the flock is destroyed. The moral at the end of the story shows that liars are not rewarded: even if they tell the truth, no one believes them.

Acknowledgements

My special thanks to SolDesign for all their artistic input and technical know-how in the creation of this book. To Stephanie Arnold for her unwavering support and crucial editorial contributions. To Joe Landry for his Salzburg friendship and guidance. To my wife and family for all their help. And to Chris Beatrice, for his illustrations and vision and believing that Maurice is a special mouse.

DRAW ON ME

DRAW ON ME

DRAW ON ME